THE FALSE GODS

By

GEORGE HORACE LORIMER

AUTHOR OF
Letters from a
Self-Made Merchant to His Son

First published in 1906

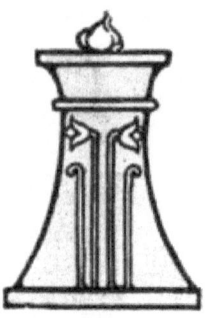

British Library Cataloguing-in-Publication Data
A catalogue record for this book is available
from the British Library

To A.V.L.

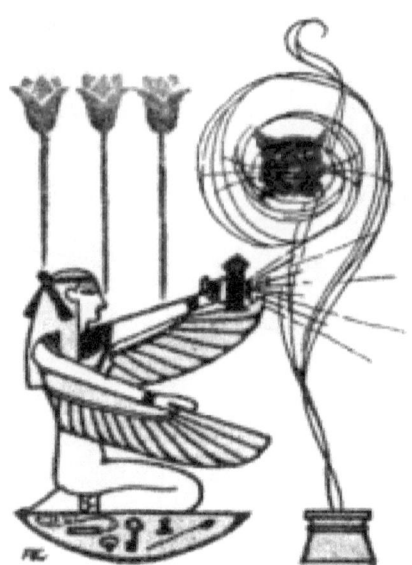

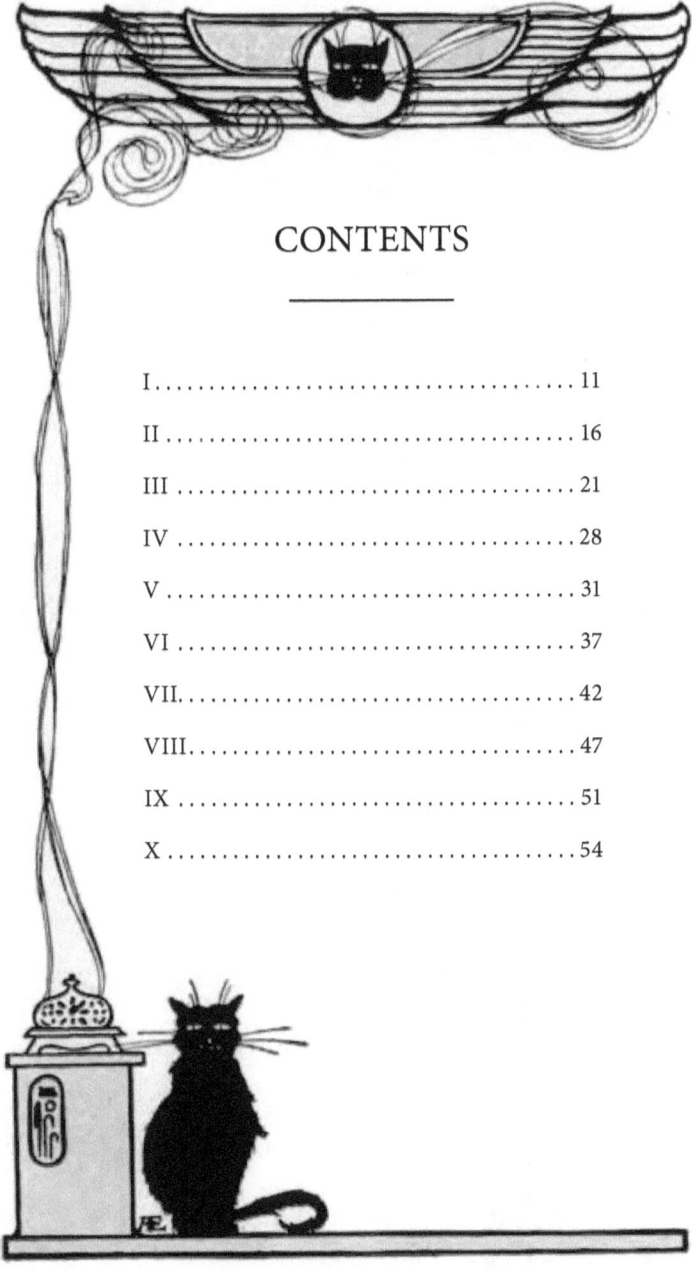

CONTENTS

ILLUSTRATIONS

GEORGE HORACE LORIMER

JAMES MONTGOMERY FLAGG

Who makes Saturday evening a big night

"Business is like oil —
it won't mix with anything but business"

"Education will broaden a narrow mind,
but there's no known cure for a big head"

"Appearances are deceitful, I know,
but so long as they are, there's nothing
like having them decieve for us instead of against us. "

'Then ... the arms crushed him against the stone breast.'

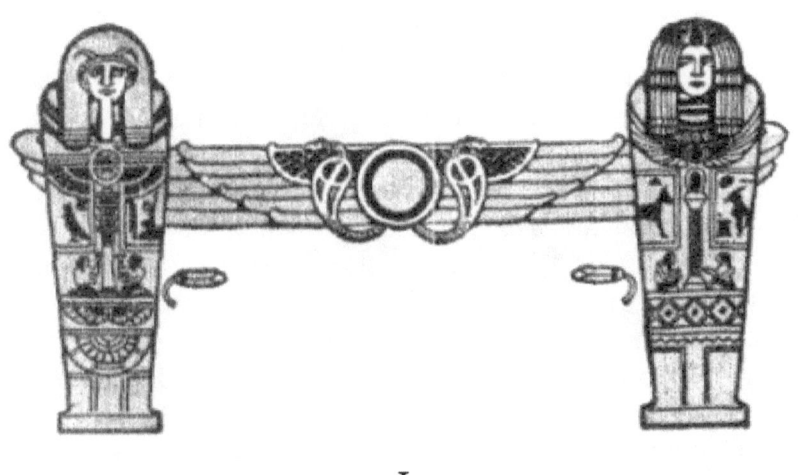

I

Simpkins regarded knocking on doors and sending in cards as formalities which served merely to tempt people of a retiring disposition to lie, so when he walked into the waiting-room and found it deserted, he passed through it quickly and opened the door beyond. But if he had expected this manœuver to bring him within easy distance of the person whom he was seeking, he was disappointed. He had simply walked into a small outer office. A self-sufficient youth of twelve, who was stuffed into a be-buttoned suit, was its sole occupant.

"Hello, bub!" said Simpkins to this Cerberus of the threshold. "Mrs. Athelstone in?" and he drew out his letter of introduction; for he had instantly decided to use it in place of a card, as being more likely to gain him admittance.

"Aw, fergit it," the youth answered with fine American independence. "I'll let youse know when your turn comes, an' youse can keep your ref'rences till you're asked for 'em," and he surveyed Simpkins with marked disfavor.

The reporter made no answer and asked no questions. Until that moment he had not known that he had a turn, but if he had,

11

he did not propose to lose it by any foolish slip. So he settled down in his chair and began to turn over his assignment in his mind.

That Simpkins had come over to New York was due to the conviction of his managing editor, Mr. Naylor, that a certain feature which had been shaping up in his head would possess a peculiar interest if it could be "led" with a few remarks by Mrs. Athelstone. Though her husband, the Rev. Alfred W.R. Athelstone, was a Church of England clergyman, whose interest in Egyptology had led him to accept the presidency of the American branch of the Royal Society, she was a leader among the Theosophists. And now that the old head of the cult was dead, it was rumored that Mrs. Athelstone had announced the reincarnation of Madame Blavatsky in her own person. This in itself was a good "story," but it was not until a second rumor reached Naylor's ears that his newspaper soul was stirred to its yellowest depths. For there was in Boston an association known as the American Society for the Investigation of Ancient Beliefs, which was a rival of the Royal Society in its good work of laying bare with pick and spade the buried mysteries along the Nile. And this rivalry, which was strong between the societies and bitter between their presidents, became acute in the persons of their secretaries, both of whom were women. Madame Gianclis, who served the Boston Society, boasted Egyptian blood in her veins, a claim which Mrs. Athelstone, who acted as secretary for her husband's society, politely conceded, with the qualification that some ancestor of her rival had contributed a dash of the Senegambian as well.

This remark, duly reported to Madame Gianclis, had not put her in a humor to concede Madame Blavatsky's soul, or any part of it, to Mrs. Athelstone. Promptly on hearing of her pretensions, so rumor had it, the Boston woman had announced the reincarnation of Theosophy's high priestess in herself. And Boston believers were inclined to accept her view, as it was difficult for them to understand how any soul with liberty of action could deliberately choose a New York residence.

"'Aw, fergit it.'

Now, all these things had filtered through to Naylor from those just without the temple gates, for whatever the quarrels of the two societies and their enemies, they tried to keep them to themselves. They had had experience with publicity and had found that ridicule goes hand in hand with it in this iconoclastic age. But out of these rumors, unconfirmed though they were, grew a vision in Naylor's brain—a vision of a glorified spread in the *Sunday Banner's* magazine section. Under a two-page "head," builded cunningly of six sizes of type, he saw ravishingly

13

beautiful pictures of Madame Gianclis and Mrs. Athelstone, and hovering between them the materialized, but homeless, soul of Madame Blavatsky, trying to make choice of an abiding-place, the whole enlivened and illuminated with much "snappy" reading matter.

Now, Simpkins was the man to make a managing editor's dreams come true, so Naylor rubbed the lamp for him and told him what he craved. But the reporter's success in life had been won by an ability to combine much extravagance of statement in the written with great conservatism in the spoken word. Early in his experience he had learned that Naylor's optimism, though purely professional, entailed unpleasant consequences on the reporter who shared it and then betrayed some too generous trust; so he absolutely refused to admit that there was any basis for it now.

"You know she won't talk to reporters," he protested. "Those New York boys have joshed that whole bunch so they're afraid to say their prayers out loud. Then she's English and dead swell, and that combination's hard to open, unless you have a number in the Four Hundred, and then it ain't refined to try. I can make a pass at her, but it'll be a frost for me."

"Nonsense! You must make her talk, or manage to be around while some one else does," Naylor answered, waving aside obstacles with the noble scorn of one whose business it is to set others to conquer them. "I want a good snappy interview, understand, and descriptions for some red-hot pictures, if you can't get photos. I'm going to save the spread in the Sunday magazine for that story, and you don't want to slip up on the Athelstone end of it. That hall is just what the story needs for a setting. Get in and size it up."

"You remember what happened to that *Courier* man who got in?" ventured Simpkins.

"I believe I did hear something about a *Courier* man's being snaked out of a closet and kicked downstairs. Served him right. *Very* coarse work. Very coarse work *indeed*. There's a better way and you'll find it." There was something unpleasantly significant in his voice, as he terminated the interview by swinging around to his desk and picking up a handful of papers, which warned the reporter that he had gone the limit.

Simpkins had heard of the hall, for it had been written up just after Doctor Athelstone, who was a man of some wealth, had assembled in it his private collection of Egyptian treasures. But he knew, too, that it had become increasingly difficult to penetrate since Mrs. Athelstone had been made the subject of some entertaining, but too imaginative, Sunday specials. Still, now that he had properly magnified the difficulties of the undertaking to Naylor, that the disgrace of defeat might be discounted or the glory of achievement enhanced, he believed that he knew a way to gain access to the hall and perhaps to manage a talk with Mrs. Athelstone herself. His line of thought started him for Cambridge, where he had a younger brother whom he was helping through Harvard.

As a result of this fraternal visit, Simpkins minor cut the classes of Professor Alexander Blackburn, the eminent archæologist, for the next week, and went to his other lectures by back streets. For the kindly professor had given him a letter, introducing him to Mrs. Athelstone as a worthy young student with a laudable thirst for that greater knowledge of Egyptian archæology, ethnology and epigraphy which was to be gained by an inspection of her collection. And it was the possession of this letter which influenced Simpkins major to take the smoking car and to sit up all night, conning an instructive volume on Ancient Egypt, thereby acquiring much curious information, and diverting two dollars of his expense money to the pocket in which he kept his individual cash balance.

II

They had stepped from the present into the past. Simpkins found himself looking between a double row of pillars, covered with hieroglyphics in red and black, to an altar of polished black basalt, guarded on either side by stone sphinxes. Behind it, straight from the lofty ceiling, fell a veil of black velvet, embroidered with golden scarabæi, and fringed with violet. The approach, a hundred paces or more, was guarded by twoscore mummies in black cases, standing upright along the pillars.

"Watcher gawkin' at?" demanded the youth, grinning up at the staring Simpkins. "Lose dat farmer-boy face or it's back to de ole homestead for youse. Her royal nibs ain't lookin' for no good milker."

"Oh, I'm just rubbering to see where the goat's kept," the reporter answered, trying to assume a properly metropolitan expression. "Suppose I'll have to take the third degree before I can get out of here."

The youth started noiselessly across the floor, and Simpkins saw that he wore sandals. His own heavy walking boots rang loudly on the flagged floors and woke the echoes in the vaulted ceiling.

He began to tread on tiptoe, as one moves in a death-chamber.

And that was what this great room was: a charnel-house filled with the spoil of tombs and temples.

The dim light fluttered down from quaint, triangular

windows, set with a checker-work of brick-red and saffron-colored panes about a central design, a scarlet heart upon a white star, and within that a black scarabæus. The white background of the walls threw into relief the angular figures on the frieze, scenes from old Egyptian life: games, marriages, feasts and battles, painted in the crude colors of early art.

Between were paneled pictures of the gods, monstrous and deformed deities, half men, half beasts; and the dado, done in black, pictured the funeral rites of the Egyptians, with explanatory passages from the ritual of the dead.

Rudely-sculptured bas-reliefs and intaglios, torn from ancient mastabas, were set over windows and doors, and stone colossi of kings and gods leered and threatened from dusky corners. Sarcophagi of black basalt, red porphyry and pink-veined alabaster, cunningly carved, were disposed as they had been found in the pits of the dead, with the sepulchral vases and the hideous wooden idols beside them.

The descriptions of the place had prepared Simpkins for something out of the ordinary, but nothing like this; and he looked about him with wonder in his eyes and a vague awe at his heart, until he found himself standing in the corner of the hall to the right of the black altar in the west.

Two sarcophagi, one of basalt, the other of alabaster, were placed at right angles to the walls, partially inclosing a small space. Within this inclosure, bowed over a stone table, sat a woman, writing. At either end of the table a mummy case, one black, the other gilt, stood upright.

The boy halted just outside this singular private office, and the woman rose and came toward them.

Simpkins had never read Virgil, but he knew the goddess by her walk. She was young—not over thirty—and tall and stately.

Her gown was black, some soft stuff which clung about her, and a bunch of violets at her waist made the whole corner faintly sweet.

Her features were regular, but of a type strange to Simpkins, the nose slightly aquiline, the lips full and red—vividly so by contrast to the clear white of the skin—and the forehead low and straight. Black hair waved back from it, and was caught up by the coils of a golden asp, from whose lifted head two rubies gleamed. Doubtless a woman would have pronounced her gown absurd and her way of wearing her hair an intolerable affectation. But it was effective with the less discriminating animal—instantly so with Simpkins.

And then she raised her eyes and looked at him. To the first glance they were dusky eyes, deep and fathomless, changing swiftly to the blue-black of the northern skies on a clear winter night, and flashing out sharp points of light, like star-rays.

He knew that in that glance he had been weighed, gauged and classed, and, though he was used to questioning Governors and Senators quite unabashed and unafraid, he found himself standing awkward and ill-at-ease in the presence of this woman.

Had she addressed him in Greek or Egyptian, he would have accepted it as a matter of course. But when she did speak it was in the soft, clear tones of a well-bred Englishwoman, and what she said was commonplace enough.

"I suppose you've called to see about the place?" she asked.

"Ye-es," stammered Simpkins, but with wit enough to know that he had come at an opportune moment. If there were a place, decidedly he had called to see about it.

"Who sent you?" she continued, and he understood that he was not there in answer to a want advertisement.

"Professor Blackburn." And he presented his letter and went on, with a return of his glibness: "You see, I've been working my way through Harvard—preparing for the ministry—Congregationalist. Found I'd have to stop and go to work regularly for a while before I could finish. So I've come over here, where I can attend the night classes at Columbia at the same time.

And as I'm interested in Egyptology, and had heard a good deal about your collection, I got that letter to you. Thought you might know some one in the building who wanted a man, as work in a place like this would be right in my line. Of course, if you're looking for any one, I'd like to apply for the place." And he paused expectantly.

"I see. You want to be a Dissenting minister, and you're working for your education. Very creditable of you, I'm sure. And you're a stranger in New York, you say?"

"Utter," returned Simpkins.

Mrs. Athelstone proceeded to question him at some length about his qualifications. When he had satisfied her that he was competent to attend to the easy, clerical work of the office and to care for the more valuable articles in the hall, things which she did not care to leave to the regular cleaners, she concluded:

"I'm disposed to give you a trial, Mr. Simpkins, but I want you to understand that under no circumstances are you to talk about me or your work outside the office. I've been so hunted and harried by reporters——" And her voice broke. "What I want above all else is a clerk that I can trust."

The assurance which Simpkins gave in reply came harder than all the lies he had told that morning, and, some way, none of them had slipped out so smoothly as usual. He was a fairly truthful and tender-hearted man outside his work, but in it he had accustomed himself to regard men and women in a purely impersonal way, and their troubles and scandals simply as material.

To his mind, nothing was worth while unless it had a news value; and nothing was sacred that had. But he was uneasily conscious now that he was doing a deliberately brutal thing, and for the first time he felt that regard for a subject's feelings which is so fatal to success in certain branches of the new journalism. But he repressed the troublesome instinct, and when Mrs. Athelstone dismissed him a few minutes later, it was with the understanding that he should report the next morning, ready for work.

He stopped for a moment in the ante-chamber on the way

out; for the bright light blinded him, and there were red dots before his eyes. He felt a little subdued, not at all like the self-confident man who had passed through the oaken door ten minutes before. But nothing could long repress the exuberant Simpkins, and as he started down the stairway to the street he was exclaiming to himself:

"Did you butt in, Simp., old boy, or were you pushed?"

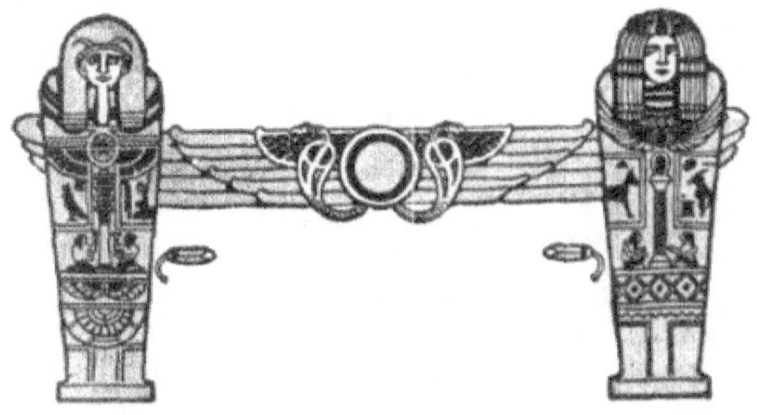

III

"If I were equal to it, I should look after these myself," she explained. "Careless hands would soon ruin this case." And she touched the gilt mummy beside her writing-table affectionately. "She was a queen, Nefruari, daughter of the King of Ethiopia. They called her 'the good and glorious woman.'"

"And this—this black boy?" questioned Simpkins respectfully. "Looks as if he might have lived during the eighteenth dynasty." He had not been poring over volumes on Ancient Egypt for two nights without knowing a thing or two about black mummies.

"Quite right, Simpkins," Mrs. Athelstone replied, evidently pleased by his interest and knowledge. "He was Amosis, a king of the eighteenth dynasty, and Nefruari's husband. A big, powerful man!"

"What a bully cigarette brand he'd make!" thought Simpkins, and aloud he added:

"They must have been a fine-looking pair."

"Indeed, yes," was the earnest answer, and so they moved about the hall, she explaining, he listening and questioning, until at last they stood before the black altar in the west and the veil of velvet. Simpkins saw that there was an inscription carved in the basalt, and, drawing nearer, slowly spelled out:

TIBI

VNA	QVE
ES	OMNIA
DEA	ISIS

"And what's behind the curtain?" he began, turning toward Mrs. Athelstone.

"The truth, of course. But remember," and her tone was half serious, "none but an adept may look behind the veil and live."

"The truth is my long suit," returned Simpkins mendaciously. "So I'll take a chance." As he spoke, the heavy velvet fell aside and disclosed a statue of a woman carved in black marble. It stood on a pedestal of bronze, overlaid with silver, and above and behind were hangings of blue-gray silk. A brilliant ray of light beat down on it. Glancing up, Simpkins saw that it shone from a crescent moon in the arched ceiling above the altar. Then his eyes came back to the statue. There was something so lifelike in the pose of the figure, something so winning in the smile of the face, something so alluring in the outstretched arms, that he involuntarily stepped nearer.

"And now that you've seen Isis, what do you think of her?" asked Mrs. Athelstone, breaking the momentary silence.

"She's the real thing—the naked truth, sure enough," returned Simpkins with a grin.

"It *is* a wonderful statue!" was the literal answer. "There's no other like it in the world. Doctor Athelstone found it near Thebes, and took a good deal of pride in arranging this shrine. The device *is* clever; the parting of the veil you see, makes the light shine down on the statue, and it dies out when I close it—so"; and, as she pulled a cord, the veil fell before the statue and the light melted away.

"'She's the Real Thing.'

"Aren't you initiating the neophyte rather early?" a man's voice asked at Simpkins' elbow, and, as he turned to see who it was, Mrs. Athelstone explained: "This is our new clerk, Mr. Simpkins; Doctor Brander is our treasurer, and our acting president while my husband's away. He left a few days ago for a little rest." And Mrs. Athelstone turned back to her desk.

Simpkins instantly decided to dislike the young clergyman beside him. He was tall and athletic-looking, but with a slight stoop, that impressed the reporter as a physical assumption of humility which the handsome face, with its faintly sneering lines and bold eyes, contradicted. But he acknowledged Brander's offhand "How d'ye do?" in a properly deferential manner, and listened respectfully to a few careless sentences of instructions.

For the rest of the morning, Simpkins mechanically addressed circulars appealing for funds to carry on the good work of the Society, while his mind was busy trying to formulate a plan by which he could get Mrs. Athelstone to tell what she knew about the whereabouts of Madame Blavatsky's soul. He felt, with the accurate instinct of one used to classing the frailties of flesh and blood according to their worth in columns, that those devices which had so often led women to confide to him the details of the particular sensation that he was working up would avail him nothing here. "You simply haven't got her Bertillon measurements, Simp.," he was forced to admit, after an hour of fruitless thinking. "You'll have to trust in your rabbit's foot."

But if Mrs. Athelstone was a new species to him, the office boy was not. He knew that youth down to the last button on his jacket. He knew, too, that an office boy often whiles away the monotonous hours by piecing together the president's secrets from the scraps in his waste-basket. So at the noon hour he slipped out after Buttons, caught him as he was disappearing up a near-by alley in a cloud of cigarette smoke, like the disreputable little devil that he was, and succeeded in establishing friendly and even familiar relations with him.

It was not, however, until late in the afternoon, when he

was called into the ante-chamber to discover the business of a caller, that he improved the opportunity to ask the youth some leading questions.

"Suppose you open up mornings?" he began carelessly.

"Naw; Mrs. A. does. She bunks here."

"How?"

"In a bed. She's got rooms in de buildin'. That door by Booker T. leads to 'em."

"Booker T.? Oh, sure! The brunette statue. And that other door—the one to the left. Where does that go?"

"Into Brander's storeroom. He sells mummies on de side."

"Does, eh? Curious business!" commented Simpkins. "Seems to rub it into *you* pretty hard. And stuck on himself! Don't seem able to spit without ringing his bell for some one to see him do it. Guess you'd have to have four legs to satisfy *him*, all right."

"Say, dat duck ain't on de level," the grievance for which Simpkins had been probing coming to the surface.

"Holds out on what he collects? Steals?"

"Sure t'ing—de loidies," and the boy lowered his voice; "he's dead stuck on Mrs. A."

"Oh! nonsense," commented Simpkins, an invitation to continue in his voice. "She's a married woman."

"Never min', I'm tellin' youse; an dat's just where de stink comes in. Ain't I seen 'im wid my own eyes a-makin' goo-goos at 'er. An' wasn't there rough house for fair goin' on in dere last mont', just before de Doc. made his get-away? He tumbled to somethin', all right, all right, or why don't he write her? Say, I don't expect *him* back in no hurry. He's hived up in South Dakote right now, an' she's in trainin' for alimony, or my name's Dennis Don'tknow."

"Does look sort of funny," Simpkins replied, sympathetic, but not too interested. "When was it Doc. left? Last week?"

"Last week, not; more'n a mont' ago, an' he ain't peeped since, for I've skinned every mail dat's come in, an' not a picture-postal, see?"

"That isn't very affectionate of Doc., but I wouldn't mention it to any one else; it might get you into trouble," was Simpkins' comment. "You better—Holy, jumping Pharaoh! what a husky pussy!" As he spoke a big black cat, with blinking, tawny eyes, sprang from the floor and curled itself up on the youth's desk. "Where'd that——"

A snarl interrupted the question; for the temptation to pull the cat's tail had proved too strong for the boy. Bowed over his desk in a fit of laughter at the result, he did not see the door behind him open, but Simpkins did. And he saw Mrs. Athelstone, her eyes blazing, spring into the room, seize the youth by the collar and shake him roughly.

"You nasty little brute!" she cried. "How dared you do that to a——" And then catching sight of Simpkins, she dropped the frightened boy back into his chair.

"I can't stand cruelty to animals," she explained, panting a little from her effort. "If anything of this sort happens again, I'll discharge you on the spot," she added to the boy.

"Shame!" Simpkins echoed warmly. "Didn't know what was up or I'd have stopped him."

"I'm sure of it," she answered graciously, and, stooping, she picked up the now purring cat and left the room.

Simpkins followed her back to his desk and went on with his addressing, but he had something worth thinking about now. Not for nothing had he been educated in that newspaper school which puts two and two together and makes six. And by the time he was through work for the day and back in his room at the hotel, he had his result. He embodied it in this letter to Naylor:

Dear Mr. Naylor:
I am in the employ of Mrs. Athelstone. How I managed it is a yarn that will keep till I get back. [He meant until he could invent the story which would reflect the most credit on his ingenuity, for though he knew that the whole thing had been a piece of luck he had no intention of cheapening himself with Naylor by owning as much.] I had intended

to return to Boston to-night, but I'm on the track of real news, a lovely stink, something much bigger than the Sunday story. There's a sporting parson, quite a swell, in the office here who's gone on Mrs. A., and I'm inclined to hope she is on him. Anyway, the Doc. left in a hurry after some sort of a row over a month ago, and hasn't written a line to his wife since. She's as cool as a cucumber about it and handed me a hot one right off the bat about poor old Doc.'s having gone away for a rest *a few days ago*. I've drawn cards and am going to sit in the game, unless you wire me to come home, for I smell a large, fat, front-page exclusive, which will jar the sensitive slats of some of our first families both here and in dear old London.
Yours,
Simpkins.

He hesitated a few minutes before he mailed the letter. He really did not want to do anything to involve *her* in a scandal, but, after all, it was simply anticipating the inevitable, and—he pulled himself up short and put the letter in the box. He could not afford any mawkish sentiment in this.

IV

She never referred, even indirectly, to her husband, but Simpkins, as he watched her move about the hall, divined that he was often in her thoughts. And there was another whom he watched—Brander; for he felt certain now that the acting president's interest in his handsome secretary was not purely that of the Egyptologist. And though there was nothing but a friendly courtesy in her manner toward him, Simpkins knew his subject well enough to understand that, whatever her real feelings were, she was far too clever to be tripped into betraying them to him. "She doesn't wear her heart on her sleeve—if she has a heart," he decided.

He was trying to make up his mind to force things to some sort of a crisis, one morning, when Mrs. Athelstone called him to her desk and said rather sharply:

"You've been neglecting your work, Simpkins. Isis looks as if she hadn't been dusted since you came."

This was the fact. Simpkins never passed the black altar without a backward glance, as if he were fearful of an attack from behind. And he had determined that nothing should tempt him to a tête-à-tête with the statue behind the veil. But having so senseless, so cowardly a feeling was one thing, and letting Mrs. Athelstone know it another. So he only replied:

"I'm very sorry; afraid I have been a little careless about the statue." And taking up a soft cloth, he walked toward the altar.

It was quite dark behind the veil; so dark that he could see nothing at first. But after the moment in which his eyes grew accustomed to the change, he made out the vague lines of the statue in the faint light from above. He set to work about the pedestal, touching it gingerly at first, then more boldly. At length he looked up into the face, blurred in the half-light.

When he had finished with the pedestal he pulled himself up between the outstretched arms, and perhaps a trifle hurriedly now, as he saw the face more distinctly, began to pass the cloth over the arms and back.

Then, quick as the strike of a snake, the arms crushed him against the stone breast. He could not move; he could not cry out; he could not breathe. The statue, seen from the level of the pedestal, had changed its whole expression. Hate glowed in its eyes; menace lived in every line of its face. The arms tightened slowly, inexorably; then, as quickly as they had closed, unclasped; and Simpkins half-slid, half-fell to the floor.

When the breath came back into his lungs and he found himself unharmed, he choked back the cry on his lips, for in that same moment a suspicion floated half-formed through his brain. He forced himself to climb up on the pedestal again, and made a careful inspection of the statue—but from behind this time.

The arms were metal, enameled to the smoothness of the body, and jointed, though the joints were almost invisible. The statue was one of those marvelous creations of the ancient priests, and once, no doubt, it had stood behind the veil in some Egyptian temple to tempt and to punish the curiosity of the neophyte.

Though Simpkins could find no clew to the mechanism of the statue, he determined that he had sprung it with his feet, and that during his struggles a lucky kick had touched the spring which relaxed the arms. "Did any one beside himself know their strength?" he asked himself, as he stepped out into the hall again. Mrs. Athelstone was bent over her desk writing; Brander was yawning over a novel in his corner, and neither paid any attention to him. So he busied himself going over the mummy-cases, and by the time he had worked around to the two beside

Mrs. Athelstone he had himself well in hand, outwardly. But he was still so shaken internally that he knocked the black case rather roughly as he dusted.

"What way is that to treat a king?" demanded Mrs. Athelstone; and the anger in her voice was so real that Simpkins, startled, blundered out:

"I really meant no disrespect. Very careless of me, I'm sure." He looked so distressed that Mrs. Athelstone's anger melted into a delicious little laugh, as she answered:

"Really, Simpkins, you musn't be so bungling. These mummies are priceless." And she got up and made a careful inspection of the case.

Simpkins, rather crestfallen, went back to his desk and began to address circulars, his brain busy with the shadow which had crept into it. But there was nothing to make it more tangible, everything to dispel it, and he was forced to own as much. "It's a lovely little cozy corner," was his final conclusion; "but keep out of it, Simp., old boy. These mechanical huggers are great stuff, but they're too strong for a fellow that's been raised on Boston girls."

V

Naylor had telegraphed that very morning: "Get story. Come home. What do you think you're doing?" and he tried to make up his mind to end the whole affair by taking the night train to Boston. But he hated to go back empty-handed from a four days' assignment. Besides, though he knew himself a fool for it, he wanted to see Mrs. Athelstone once more.

So it happened that he was lingering on in the outer office when the postman threw the afternoon mail on the desk. Simpkins was alone at the moment, and he ran over the letters carelessly until he came to one addressed to Brander in Mrs. Athelstone's writing. The blue card of the palace car company was in a corner of the envelope.

"Why the deuce is she writing that skunk before she's well out of town?" he thought, scanning the envelope with jealous eyes. Then he held it up to the light, but the thick paper told nothing of what was within. Frowning, he laid the letter down, fingered it, withdrew his itching hand, hesitated, and finally put it in his pocket.

Simpkins went straight from the office to his hotel, for, though he told himself that the letter contained some instructions which Mrs. Athelstone had forgotten to give Brander before leaving, he was anxious to see just how those instructions were worded. Alone in his little room, he ripped open the letter and ran over its two pages with bewilderment growing in his face. He finished by throwing it down on the table and exclaiming helplessly: "Well, I'll be damned!"

The first sheet, without beginning or ending, contained only a line in Mrs. Athelstone's handwriting, reading: "I had to leave in such a hurry that I missed seeing you."

There was not an intelligible word on the second sheet; it was simply a succession of scrawls and puerile outline pictures, such as a child might have drawn.

To Simpkins' first aggrieved feeling that his confidence had been abused, the certainty that he had stumbled on something of importance quickly succeeded. He concluded a second and more careful scrutiny of the letter with the exclamation, "Cipher! all right, all right," and, after a third, he jumped up excitedly and rushed off to Columbia University.

An hour later, Professor Ashmore, whose well-known work on "Hieratic Writings" is so widely accepted an authority on that fascinating subject, looked across to Simpkins, who for some minutes had been sitting quietly in a corner of his study, and observed dryly:

"This is a queer jumble of hieroglyphics and hieratic writing, and is not, I should judge," and his eyes twinkled, "of any great antiquity."

"Quite right, Professor," Simpkins assented cheerfully. "The lady who wrote it is interested in Egyptology, and is trying to have a little fun with me."

"If I may judge from the letter, she seems to be interested in you as well," the professor went on smilingly. "In fact, it appears to be—ahem—a love-letter."

"Eh! What?" exclaimed Simpkins, suddenly serious, "Let's have it."

"Well, roughly, it goes something like this: 'My heart's dearest, my sun, my Nile duck—the hours are days without thee, the days an æon. The gods be thanked that this separation is not for long. For apart from thee I have no life. That thing that I have to do is about done. May the gods guard thee and the all-mother protect thee. I embrace thee: I kiss thine eyes and thy lips.' That's a fair translation, though one or two of the hieroglyphics are susceptible of a slightly different rendering; but the sense would not be materially affected by the change," the Professor concluded.

His words fell on inattentive ears; for Simpkins was sitting stunned under the revelation of the letter. Now that he had his story, he knew that he had not wanted it.

But he roused himself when he became conscious that the professor was peering at him curiously over the top of his glasses, and said:

"Pretty warm stuff, eh! Good josh! Great girl! Ought to know her. She's daft on this Egyptian business."

"Her letter is perhaps a trifle er—impulsive," the professor answered. "But she combines the ancient and the modern charmingly. I congratulate you."

"Thanks, Professor," Simpkins answered awkwardly, and took his leave.

Once in the street, he plunged along, head down. It was worse than he had suspected. He had felt all along that the boy's surmises about Brander were correct; now he knew that his suspicions of Mrs. Athelstone were well founded. But he would keep her from that hypocrite, that hawk, that—murderer! Simpkins stopped short at the intrusion of that word. It had come without logic or reason, but he knew now that it had been shaping in his head for two days past. And once spoken, it began to justify itself. There was the motive, clear, distinct and proven; there were the means and the man.

Next morning Simpkins was earlier than usual at the Oriental Building, where he found the youth waiting for Brander to come and open up the inner office.

"Parson's late, eh?" he threw out by way of greeting.

"Always is," was the surly answer. "He's de 'rig'nal seven sleepers."

"Puts you behind with your cleaning, eh?"

"Naw; youse ought to know I don't do no cleanin'."

"You don't? I thought you tended to Mrs. Athelstone's rooms and—Mr. Brander's storeroom."

"Aw, go wan. I'm no second girl, an' de storeroom's never cleaned. Dere's nothin' to clean but a lot of stones an' bum mummies an' such."

"Brander can't sell much stuff; I never see anything being shipped."

"Oh! I don't know! We sent a couple of embammed dooks to Chicago last week."

"And last month?"

"Search me; I only copped out me job here last mont'; but seems as if his whiskers did say dere was somethin' doin'." And just then Mr. Brander came along.

Simpkins had found out what he wanted to know, and he decided that he must bring his plans to a head at once. Mrs. Athelstone was expected back the next day; he must search the storeroom that very night. If—well, he thought he could spoil one scoundrel.

He worked to good advantage during the day, and at nine o'clock that night, when he was back outside the Oriental Building, there were three new keys in his pocket.

He unlocked the door noiselessly, tiptoed up the staircase, and gained the friendly blackness of the ante-chamber quite unobserved. The watchman was half a block away, sitting by the only street entrance kept open at night.

Simpkins took off his shoes and found his sandals without striking a light, and then felt his way to the door leading into the hall. The knob rattled a little under his hand. All that evening he had been nerving himself to go in there alone and in the dark, but now he could have turned and run like a country boy passing a graveyard at night.

The hall was not utterly black, as he had expected. Light from the electric lamps without flickered through the stained-glass windows. Ghastly rays of yellow played over the painted faces on the walls and lit up the gilded features of the mummy by Mrs. Athelstone's desk. There were crimson spots, like blotches of blood, on the veil of Isis. And all about were moving shadows, creeping forward stealthily, falling back slowly, as the light without flared up or died down.

Step by step Simpkins advanced on the black altar, his muscles rigid, his nerves quivering, his eyes staring straight ahead, as a child stares into the dark for some awful shape which it fears to see, yet dares not leave unseen. Once past that altar he would be safe at the door of the storeroom.

How his heart was beating! He was almost at it. Steady! A few steps now and he would gain the storeroom. Good God! What was that!

In the blackness behind the altar two eyes flamed.

Simpkins stopped; he was helpless to turn or to advance. Perhaps if he did not move, it would not. A moment he stood there, tense with terror, then—straight from the altar the thing flew at his throat. But quick as it was: the involuntary jerk of his arm upward was quicker, and it received the blow. Snarling, the thing fell to the floor, and leaped back into the darkness. It was Mrs. Athelstone's cat.

So strong was Simpkins' revulsion of feeling, so great his relief, that he forgot the real cause of his terror, and sank down on the very steps of the altar, weakly exclaiming over and over again: "Only the cat! Only the cat! Great Scott! how it frightened me!"

He had been sitting there for a few minutes when he heard a soft click, click, just to his right. Some one was turning a key in the door leading from Mrs. Athelstone's apartments. As he jumped to his feet, he heard a hand grasp the doorknob. He looked around for a hiding-place, ran a few steps from the altar, doubled like a baited rat, and dove into the blackness behind the veil of Isis. There had been no time to choose; for hardly was he safe under cover and peeping out from between the folds of the veil than the door swung open slowly.

VI

For an uncertain moment she stood just within the hall, bathed in the light that shone through from her apartments. Then she closed the door and walked toward the veil. As she came through the shafts of light from the windows, her gown was stained with crimson spots. She was at the altar now, and Simpkins could no longer see her without changing his position. Stealthily he edged along, careless of the statue just behind him. As he parted the folds of the veil he saw that the altar was heaped with flowers. Just beyond, the light playing fantastically on her upturned face, stood Mrs. Athelstone.

Simpkins closed the veil abruptly. There came to him the remembrance of the time when the boy had pulled the cat's tail, her anger and her curious exclamation; and again, the repetition of it in his case, when he had handled the mummy of Amosis roughly; and her affectation of Egyptian symbols as ornaments. "She's the simon-pure Blavatsky, all right," he concluded, as he pieced these things into what he had just seen. "All others are base imitations."

The reporter had gathered from his little reading that behind these monstrous gods and this complex symbolism there was something near akin to Christianity in a few great essentials, and he understood how a woman of Mrs. Athelstone's temperament, engrossed in the study of these things and living in these surroundings, might be affected by them. Even he, shrewd, hard Yankee that he was, had felt the influence of the place, and there was that behind him then which made his heart beat quicker at the thought.

When he looked out again Mrs. Athelstone was gone. He was impatient to get to his work in the storeroom; but first he peeped out again to make sure that she had returned to her room. She was still in the hall, walking about in the corner where she ordinarily worked. There was something methodical in her movements now that woke a new interest in Simpkins. "What the dickens can she be up to?" he thought.

She had lit a lamp, and had shaded it, so that its rays were contracted in a circle on the floor. From a cupboard let into the wall she was taking bottles and brushes, a roll of linen bandages and some boxes of pigments. After laying these on the floor, she walked over to the big black mummy case by her table, and pushed until she had turned it around with its face to the wall.

What heathen game was this? Simpkins' interest increased, and he poked his head out boldly from the sheltering veil.

Mrs. Athelstone was standing directly in front of the case now, pulling and tugging in an effort to bring it down on her shoulders. Finally, she managed to tilt it toward her, and then, straining, she lowered it until it rested flat on the floor.

"Sorry I couldn't have lent a hand," thought the gallant Simpkins; "the old buck must weigh a ton. Now what's she bothering around that passé, three-thousand-years-dead sport for?"

Her back was toward him; so, cautious and catlike, he stole from behind the veil and glided to the shelter of a post not ten feet from her. He peered around it eagerly. Still panting from her efforts, she was on her knees beside the case, fumbling a key in the Yale lock, a curious anachronism which Simpkins, in his cleaning, had found on all the more valuable mummy cases.

The lid was of sycamore wood, comparatively light, and she lifted it without trouble. Then the rays of the lamp shone full into the open case, and Simpkins looked over the shoulders of the kneeling woman at the mummy of a man who had stood full six feet in life. He stared long at the face, seeking in those shriveled features a reason for the horror which grew in him as he gazed, trying to build back into life again that thing which once had been a man. For there was something about it which seemed different from those Egyptians of whom he had read. Slowly the vaguely-familiar features filled out, until Simpkins saw—not the swarthy, low-browed face of an Egyptian king, but the ruddy, handsome face of an Englishman, and—at last he was sure, a face like that of a photograph in his pocket. And in that same moment there went through his mind a sentence from the curious picture letter: "*That thing that I have to do is about done.*"

Already, in his absorption, he had started out from the shelter of the pillar, and now he crept forward. He was almost on her, and she had heard nothing, seen nothing, but suddenly she felt him coming, and turned. And as her eyes, full of fear in the first startled consciousness of discovery, met his, he sprang at her, and pinioned her arms to her side. But only for a moment. Fear fought with her, and by a mighty effort she half shook herself free.

Simpkins found himself struggling desperately now to regain his advantage. Already his greater strength was telling, when the lamp crashed over, leaving them in darkness, and he felt the blow of a heavy body striking his back. Claws dug through his clothes, deep into his flesh. Something was at his head now, biting and tearing, and the warm blood was trickling down into his eyes. A stealthy paw reached round for his throat. He could feel its silken surface passing over his bare flesh, the unsheathing of its steel to strike, and, as it sank into his throat, he seized it, loosening, to do this, his hold on Mrs. Athelstone, quite careless of her in the pain and menace of that moment.

Still clutching the great black cat, though it bit and tore at his hands, he gained his feet. In the darkness he could see nothing but two blazing eyes, and not until the last spark died in them did his fingers relax. Then, with a savage joy, he threw the limp body against the altar of Isis, and turned to see what had become of Mrs. Athelstone. She lay quite still where he had left her, a huddled heap of white upon the floor.

"Suddenly she felt him coming, and turned.

Simpkins righted and lit the overturned lamp and lifted the unconscious woman into a chair. There he bound her, wrapping her about with the linen bandages, until she was quite helpless to move. The obsidian eyes of the mummy seemed to follow him as he went about his task. Annoyed by their steady regard, he threw a cloth over the face and sat down to wait for the woman to come back to life.

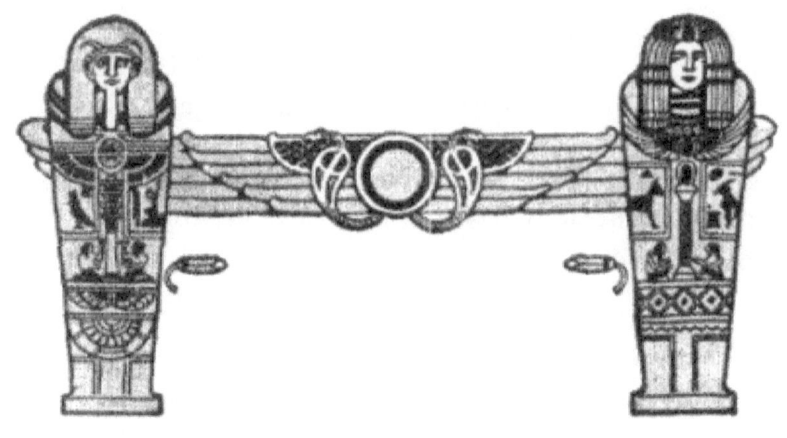

VII

He looked at his watch anxiously. He had plenty of time—the paper did not go to press until two. Relieved, he glanced toward Mrs. Athelstone again. How still she was! She was taking an unreasonably long time about coming to! The shadows in the room began to creep in on him again, and to oppress him with a vague fear, now that he was sitting inactive. He got up, but just then the woman stirred, and he settled down again.

Slowly she recovered consciousness and looked about her. Her eyes sought out Simpkins last, and as they rested on him a flash of anger lit them up. Simpkins returned their stare unflinchingly. They had quite lost their power over him.

"So you're a thief, Simpkins—and I thought you looked so honest," she began at last, contempt in her voice.

"Not at all," Simpkins answered, relieved and grateful that she had only suspected him of being a thief, that there had been no tears, no pleadings, no hysterics; "I'm nothing of the sort. I'm just your clerk."

"Then, what are you doing here at this time of night? And why did you attack me? Why have you bound me?"

"I'll be perfectly frank, Mrs. Athelstone." (Simpkins always prefaced a piece of duplicity by asseverating his innocence of guile.) "I've blundered on something in there," and he motioned vaguely toward the coffin, "that is reason enough for binding you and turning you over to the police, sorry as I should be to take such a step."

"And that something?"

"The body of your husband."

"You beastly little cad," began Mrs. Athelstone, anger flaming in her face again. Then she stopped short, and her expression went to one of terror.

The change was not lost on Simpkins. "That's better," he said. "If a fellow has to condone murder to meet your standards of what's a perfect little gentleman, you can count me out. Now, just you make up your mind that repartee won't take us anywhere, and let's get down to cases. There may be, I believe there are, extenuating circumstances. Tell him the whole truth and you'll find Simp. your friend, cad or no cad."

As he talked, Mrs. Athelstone regained her composure, and when he was through she asked calmly enough: "And because you've blundered on something you don't understand, something that has aroused your silly suspicions, you would turn me over to the police?"

"It's not a silly suspicion, Mrs. Athelstone, but a cinch. I know your husband was murdered there," and he pointed to the altar. "And you're not innocent, though how guilty morally I'm not ready to say. There may be something behind it all to change my present determination; that depends on whether you care to talk to me, or would rather wait and take the third degree at headquarters."

"But you really have made a frightful mistake," she protested, not angrily now, but rather soothingly.

"Then I'll have to call an officer; perhaps he can set us straight." And he stood up.

"Sit down," she implored. "Let me explain."

"That's the way to talk; you'll find it'll do you good to loosen up," and Simpkins sat down, exulting that he was not to miss the most striking feature of his story. Until it was on the wire for Boston, and the New York papers had gone to press, he had as little use for officers as Mrs. Athelstone. "Remember," he added, as he leaned back to listen, "that I know enough now to pick out any fancy work."

"It's really absurdly simple. The cemented surface of this mummy had been damaged, as you can see"——Mrs. Athelstone began, but Simpkins broke in roughly:

"Come, come, there's no use doping out any more of that stuff to me. I want the facts. Tell me how Doctor Athelstone was killed or the Tombs for yours." He was on his feet now, shaking his fist at the woman, and he noticed with satisfaction that she had shrunk back in her chair till the linen bandages hung loosely across her breast.

"Yes—yes—I'll tell," was the trembling answer; "only do sit down," and then after a moment's pause, in which she seemed to be striving to compose herself, she began:

"I, sir, was a queen, Nefruari, whom they called the good and glorious woman." And she threw back her head proudly and paused.

This was better than he had dared hope. Yet it was what he had half-believed; she was quite mad. He felt relieved at this final proof of it. After all, it would have hurt him to send this woman to "the chair"; but there would be no condemned cell for her; only the madhouse.

It might be harder for her; but it made it easier for him. He nodded a grave encouragement for her to continue.

"This is my mummy," she went on, nodding toward the gilded case, "the shell from which my soul fled three thousand years ago. Since then it has been upon its wanderings, living in birds and beasts, that the will of Osiris might be done."

Again she paused, pleased, apparently, with the respectful interest which Simpkins showed.

And, indeed, he was interested; for his reading on early Egyptian beliefs enabled him to follow the current of her madness and to trace it back to its sources. So he nodded again, and she continued:

"Through all these weary centuries, Amosis, my husband, has been with me, first as king—ah! those days in hundred-gated Thebes—and when at last my soul lodged in this body he found me out again. As boy and girl we loved, as man and woman we were married. And the days that followed were as happy as those old days when we ruled an empire. Not that we remembered then. The memory of it all but just came back to me two months ago."

"Did you tell the Doctor about it?" asked Simpkins, in the wheedling tone of a physician asking a child to put out her tongue.

"I tried to stir his memory gently, by careless hints, a word dropped here and there, recalling some bright triumph of his reign, some splendid battle, but there was no response. And so I waited, hoping that of itself his memory might quicken, as mine had."

"Did Brander know anything about this—er—extraordinary swapping around of souls?"

"Not then——" began the woman, but Simpkins cut her short by jumping to his feet with a cry of "What's that!" and his voice was sharp with fear.

For in that silent second, while he waited for her answer, he had heard a noise out in the hall, the sound of stealthy feet behind the veil, and he had seen the woman's eyes gleam triumph.

Again the terror that had mastered him an hour before leaped into life, and quakingly he faced the darkness. But he saw nothing—only the shifting shadows, the crimson blotches crawling on the veil, and the vague outlines of the coffined dead.

He looked back to the woman. Her face was masklike.

It must have been a fancy, a vibration of his own tense nerves. But none the less, he rearranged the light, that while its rays shone clear on Mrs. Athelstone, he might be in the shadow, and set his chair back close against the wall, that both the woman and the hall might be well in his eye. And when he sat down again one hand clutched tight the butt of a revolver.

VIII

"I thought I heard a slight noise, as if something were moving behind me. Perhaps a mummy was breaking out of its case," he answered, but his voice was scarcely steady enough for the flippancy of his speech.

"Hardly that," was the serious answer; "but it might have been my cat, Rameses."

"Not unless it was Rameses II., because—well, it didn't sound like a cat," he wound up, guiltily conscious of his other reason for certainty on this point. "Perhaps Isis has climbed down from her pedestal to stretch herself," and he smiled, but his eyes were anxious, and he shot a furtive glance toward the veil.

"It's hardly probable," was the calm reply.

"What? Can't the thing use its legs as well as its arms?"

"Ah! then you know——"

"Yes; she reached for me when I was dusting her off, but I kicked harder than Doctor Athelstone, I suppose, and so touched the spring twice."

"You beast!"

"Well, let it go at that," Simpkins assented. "And let's hear the rest." He was burning with impatience to reach the end and get away, back to noisy, crowded Broadway.

But Mrs. Athelstone answered nothing, only looked off toward the altar. It almost seemed as if she waited for something.

"Go on," commanded Simpkins, stirred to roughness by his growing uneasiness.

"You will not leave while yet you may?" and her tone doubled the threat of her words.

"No, not till I've heard it all," he answered doggedly, and gripped the butt of his revolver tighter. But though he told himself that her changed manner, this new confidence, this sudden indifference to his going, was the freak of a madwoman, down deep he felt that it portended some evil thing for him, knew it, and would not go, could not go; for he dared not pass the ambushed terror of that altar.

"You still insist?" the woman asked with rising anger. "So be it. Learn then the fate of meddlers, of dogs who dare to penetrate the mysteries of Isis."

Simpkins took his eyes from her face and glanced mechanically toward the veil. But he looked back suddenly, and caught her signalling with a swift motion of her head to something in the darkness. There could be no mistake this time. And following her eyes he saw a form, black and shapeless, steal along to the nearest post.

Revolver in hand, he leaped up and back, upsetting his chair. The thing remained hidden. He cleared the partitioning sarcophagus at a bound, and, sliding and backing, reached the centre of the hall, never for one instant taking his eyes from that post or lowering his revolver. Step by step, back between the pillars, he retreated, stumbling toward the door and safety.

Half-way, he heard the woman hiss: "Stop him! Don't let him escape!" And he saw the thing dart from behind the post. In the uncontrollable madness of his fear he hurled, instead of firing, his revolver at it, and turned and ran.

Tapping lightly on the flags behind, he heard swift feet. It was coming, it was gaining, but he was at the door, through it and had slammed it safely behind him. A leap, a bound, and he was through the ante-chamber, and, as the door behind him opened, he was slipping out into the passageway. He went down the stairs in great jumps. Thank God! he had left the street door unlocked. But already the sound of pursuit had stopped, and he reached the open air safely.

Down the deserted street to Broadway he ran. There he hailed a cab and directed the driver to the telegraph office. Then he leaned back and looked at the garish lights, the passing cabs, the theatre crowds hurrying along home, laughing and chatting as if the world held no such horror as that which he had just escaped. That madwoman's words rang through his brain, drowning out the voices of the street; the tapping of those flying feet sounded in his ears above the rattle of the cab. That or this must be unreal; yet how far off both seemed!

Gradually the rough jolting of the cab shook him back to a sense of his surroundings and their safety. He began to regain his nerve, and to busy himself knotting the strands of the story into a connected narrative. And when, a few minutes later, he handed a message to the manager of the telegraph office and demanded a clear wire into the *Banner* office, he was quite the old breezy Simpkins.

Then, coat off, a cigar between his teeth, he sat down beside the operator and began to write his story, his flying fingers keeping time with the clicking instrument. He made no mention of the fears that had beset him in the hall and the manner of his exit from it. But there was enough and to spare of the dramatic in what he sent. After a sensational half-column of introduction, fitting the murder on Mrs. Athelstone, and enlarging on the certainty of one's sin finding one out, provided it were assisted by a *Banner* reporter, he swung into the detailed story, dwelling on the woman's madness and sliding over the details of the murder as much as possible.

Then he described how, for more than a month, Mrs Athelstone had labored over the body, hiding it days in the empty case and dragging it out nights, until she had finished it, with the exception of some detail about the head, into a faithful replica of the mummy of Amosis, the original of which she had no doubt burned. It all made a vivid story; for never had his imagination been in such working order, and never had it responded more generously to his demands upon it. About two in the morning he finished his third column and concluded his story with:

"So this awful confession of madness and murder ended. I left the woman bound and helpless, sitting in her chair, her victim at her feet, to wait the coming of the police." Then he added to Naylor personally, "Going notify police headquarters now and go back to hall."

Naylor, who had been reading the copy page by page as it came from the wire, and who, naturally, was taking a mere cold-blooded view of the case than Simpkins, telegraphed back:

"What share did Brander have in actual murder? You don't bring that out in story."

"Couldn't get it out of her," Simpkins sent back, truthfully enough.

"Find out," was the answer. "Get back to hall quick. Brander may have looked in to help Mrs. A. with her night work while you were gone. Will hold enough men for an extra."

Simpkins called a cab and started for police headquarters at breakneck speed, but on the way he stopped at Brander's rooms; for a miserable suspicion was growing in his brain. "If that really was Isis," he was thinking, "it's funny she didn't nail me before I got to the door, even with the start I had."

On his representation that he had called on a matter of life and death, the janitor admitted him to Brander's rooms. They were empty, and the bed had not been slept in.

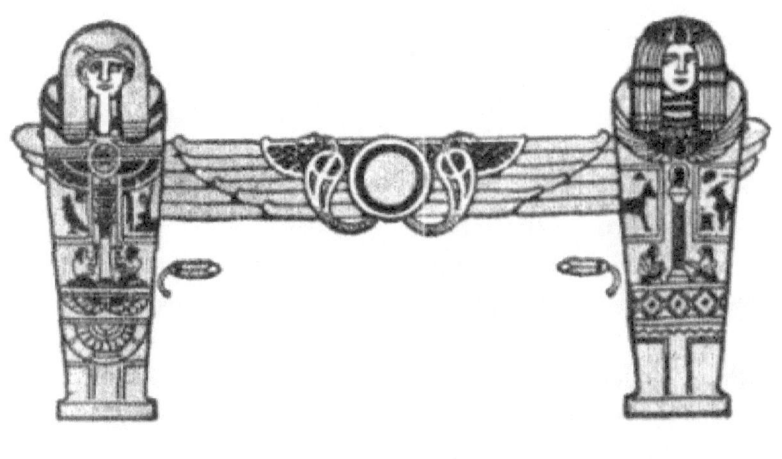

IX

There they were halted, for Simpkins had left his key sticking in the spring lock inside and slammed the door behind him, a piece of carelessness over which the officers were greatly exercised; for he had not confided to them that he had started off in a hurry. In the end, they sent the door crashing in with their shoulders and preceded Simpkins—and he was scrupulously polite about this—into the ante-chamber.

There an incandescent lamp over the youth's desk gave them light and Simpkins momentary relief. The men used hard language when they found the second door in the same condition as the first, but Simpkins took their rating meekly. They tried their shoulders again, but the oak was stout and long withstood their assaults. When at last it yielded it gave way suddenly, and they all tumbled pell-mell into the hall. Simpkins jumped up with incredible agility, and was back in the lighted ante-chamber before the others had struggled to their feet. Suddenly they stopped swearing. They looked around them. Then they, too, stepped back into the ante-chamber.

"Ain't there any way of lighting this place?" asked one of them

51

rather sullenly.

"Nothing but three incandescents over the desks," answered Simpkins.

"Use your lantern then, Tom; come on now, young feller, and show us where this woman is," he said roughly, and he pushed Simpkins through the door.

As the officers followed him, he fell back between them and linked his arms through theirs. And silently they advanced on the altar, a grotesque and rather unsteady trio, the bull's eyes on either side flashing ahead into the darkness.

"The lamp's still burning," whispered Simpkins. They were far enough into the hall now to see the glow from it in the corner. "Flash your lights around those pillars, boys. There, over there!"

The bull's eyes jumped about searching her out. "There! now! Hold still!" cried Simpkins as they focused on the chair.

The black mummy lay as he had left it, the cloth still on the face, but the chair was empty. Straight to the veil the reporter ran, and pulled the cord. Light broke from above, and beat down on an altar heaped with dying roses and the statue of a woman, smiling. And at her feet there crouched a great black cat, that arched its back and snarled at Simpkins.

Beyond, the lights were still burning in Mrs. Athelstone's apartment, but there was no one in the rooms. Some opened drawers in the bureau and the absence of her toilet articles from the table told of preparations for a hasty flight.

They did not linger long over their examination of the rooms. But after replacing the broken doors as best they could and sealing them, they went out by the main entrance to question the watchman, whom they found dozing in his chair.

Had he seen anything of Mrs. Athelstone?

Sure; he'd called a cab for her about an hour ago and she'd driven off with her brother.

"Her brother!" echoed Simpkins.

"Yep," yawned the watchman; "you know him—parson— Doctor Brander.

What's up?"

"Nothing," Simpkins returned sourly, but to himself he added, "Oh, hell!"

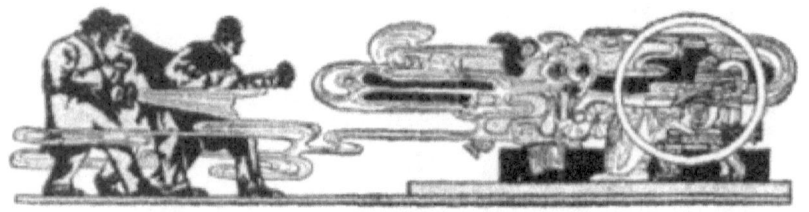

X

Of course, this sickening brother and sister business wouldn't touch the main fact of the story, but it knocked the "love motive" and the "heart interest" higher than a kite, utterly ruining some of his prettiest bits of writing, besides letting him in for a call-down from Naylor. Still, the old man couldn't be very hard on him—he'd understand that some trifling little inaccuracies were bound to creep into a great big story like this, dug out and worked up by one man.

At this more cheerful conclusion, a newsboy, crying his bundle of still damp papers, came along, and Simpkins hailed him eagerly. Standing under a lamp on the corner, skipping from front page to back, then from head to head inside, with an eye skilled to catch at a glance the stories which a loathed contemporary had that the *Banner* had missed, he ran through the bunch. The *Sun*—not a line about Athelstone in it. Bully! The *American*—he was a little afraid of the *American*. Safe again. The *World*—Sam Blythe's humorous descriptive story of the convention led. He stopped to pity Sam and the New York papers, as he thought of the Boston newsboys, crying his magnificent beat, till all Washington Street rang with the glory of it. And he could see the fellows in Mrs. Atkinson's, letting their coffee grow cold as they devoured the *Banner*, stopping only here and there to call across to each other: "Good work, Simp., old boy! Great story!"

Then—Simpkins turned the page. Accident—ten killed—

bank robbed—caught—Mrs. Jones gets divorce.... What!

NOTED SCIENTIST SECURES
IMPORTANT RIGHTS
DOCTOR ATHELSTONE ARRANGES
FOR ROYAL SOCIETY TO EXPLOIT RECENT
DISCOVERIES

Simpkins stuttered around for an exclamation; then looked up weakly. Instinct started him on the run for the nearest long-distance telephone, but before he had gone twenty feet he stopped. The paper was long since off press and distributed. He had no desire to know what Naylor was saying. He could not even guess. There are heights to which the imagination cannot aspire.

Then came a faint ray of hope. That was an Associated Press dispatch—a late one probably. But if it had reached the New York papers in time to catch the edition, Naylor must have received it soon enough to kill his story. But even as this hope came it went. The news interest of the dispatch was largely local. Doubtless it had been sent out only to the New York papers.

Simpkins forced himself to read the body of the message now, although he gagged over every line of it:

> London, etc. Dr. Alfred W.R. Athelstone, well known in London as the president of the American branch of the Royal Society of Egyptian Exploration and Research, arrived here this morning and is stopping at the Carlton. He announces that the Khedive has been graciously pleased to grant to his society the sole right to excavate the tombs recently discovered by one of its agents in the Karnak region. Doctor Athelstone left home quietly some weeks ago, and held back any announcement of the discoveries, which promise to be very important, while the negotiations, now brought to a happy conclusion, were pending. He sails for New York on the Campania tomorrow.

"Do I go off half-cocked? Am I yellow? Is a pup yellow?" groaned Simpkins, and he started off aimlessly toward the park, fighting his Waterloo over again and counting up his losses. That foolish, foolish letter! Why had he soiled his fingers by opening it! Of course, that line which loomed so large and fine in his story, that pointed the impressive finger of Fate at Crime, "*That thing that I have to do is about done!*" referred to Doctor Athelstone's silly negotiations. The letter must have been from him. Now, who could have known that a grown man would indulge in such fool monkey-business as writing love-letters in hieroglyphics to his own wife?... And that blame black mummy. Back to darkest Africa for his! If any one ever said mummy to him there'd be murder done, all right. Oh, for the happy ignorance of those days when he knew nothing about Egypt except that it was the place from which the cigarettes came!... Brander, no doubt, had gone out to send a cablegram of congratulation to Doctor Athelstone, and while he was away the woman had started in to repair a crack in that precious old Amosis of hers. Perhaps the moths had got into him! "And she thought that I was crazy, and was stringing me along, waiting till the Nile Duck got back," muttered the reporter, stopping short in his agony. "Oh! you're guessing good now, Simp., all right, because there's only one way to guess." And as he started along again he concluded: "Damn it! even the cat came back!"

If there was one thing in all the world that Simpkins did not want to see it was a copy of the *Banner* with that awful story of his staring out at him from the first page, headed and played up with all the brutal skill in handling type of which Naylor was a master; but he felt himself drawn irresistibly to the Grand Central Station, where the Boston papers would first be put on sale.

Half an hour to wait. Gad! He could never go back and face Naylor!... Libel! Why, there wasn't money enough in the world to pay the damages the Athelstones would get against the paper. He'd take just one look at it and then catch the first train for Chicago. Perhaps he could get a job there digging sewers, or selling ribbons in Fields', or start a school of journalism. Any old thing, if they didn't nab him and put him in Bloomingdale before he could get away.... He made for the street again. He wouldn't look at the *Banner*. What malignant little devils the types were when they shouted your sins, not another fellow's, from the front page, or whispered them in a stage aside from some little paragraph in an obscure corner of the paper—a corner that the whole world looked into. Hell, he'd get out of the filthy business! Think of the light and frolicsome way in which he'd written up domestic scandals, the entertaining specials he'd turned out on unfaithful husbands, the snappy columns on unhappy wives, careless of the cost of his sensation in blood and tears! And now they'd write him up—Naylor would attend to that editorial himself, and do it in his most virtuous style—and brand him as a fakir, a liar, and a yellow dog.

Simpkins was back at the news-stand again and there were the Boston papers. He snatched a *Banner* from the top of the pile. No, he must have the wrong paper. He tore through it from front to back and then to front again, his heart bounding with joy. There was not a line of his story in it. They had received that Associated Press dispatch, after all. Yes, there it was, but oh, how differently it looked! It spelt damnation an hour ago, it meant salvation now.

* * * * *

After all, hadn't his mistake been a natural one? Hadn't he done his best for the paper? Wasn't it his duty to run down a lead like that? He'd made errors of judgment, perhaps, but he'd like to see the man who wouldn't have under the circumstances. Of course, mistakes would creep in occasionally and give innocent people the worst of it, but look at the good he'd done in his life by exposing scoundrels. How could he, how could any man, have acted differently who was loyal to his paper, whose first interests were the public good? If Naylor didn't appreciate a star man when he had him, he thought he knew an editor or two who did. Simp., old boy, wasn't going to starve.... Starve? It had been hungry work, so he'd just step across to the Manhattan, get a bite of breakfast, and look up the trains to Boston.

Naylor did know a good man when he had him, and likewise— quite as valuable a bit of knowledge—he knew when a man had had enough. So when Simpkins sat down that afternoon to tell him his experiences, he only smiled quizzically as the reporter wound up by asking, "Now, what do *you* think?" and answered:

"Well, for one thing, I think it did you a power of good to look behind that veil, because I reckon that for once in your life you've told me the truth as near as you know how."

"No, but aside from this pleasant personal conclusion," persisted Simpkins, modestly shedding the compliment.

"Well, I guess we won't bother with the Blavatsky story just now, but here's a clipping about a woman who's discovered what she calls soul aura—says we've got red, white and blue souls and all that sort of stuff. You're our soul expert now, so go over to the City Hall and ask the mayor and any politicians you meet what's the color of their souls. It ought to make a fair Sunday special." And Naylor swung around to his desk, for the city editor had just told him that the headless trunk of a woman had been picked up in the river—a find that promised a good story—and a newspaper man cannot waste time on yesterday.

Simpkins' face fell. That he had not been assigned to find the head was, he knew, the beginning of his punishment. But as he walked down the dingy hall to the street his step became more buoyant, and once in the open air he started off eager and smiling. For a good opening sentence was already shaping in his head, and as he stepped into the City Hall he was repeating to himself:

"Yesterday, when the Mayor was asked, 'What is the color of your soul?' he returned his stereotyped 'Nothing to give out on that subject,' and then added, 'But it would be violating no confidence to tell you that Boss Coonahan's is black.'"

To Simpkins it had been given to lift the veil and to know the truth; yet he was back again serving the false gods.